The Strongest Thing

When Home Feels Hard

Hallee Adelman

illustrated by **Rea Zhai**

Albert Whitman & Company
Chicago, Illinois

To Alan, Lyndsey, SF, and anyone
searching for the strongest thing—HA

To my mother, who looks out for
me no matter what—RZ

Library of Congress Cataloging-in-Publication data
is on file with the publisher.

Text copyright © 2022 by Hallee Adelman
Illustrations copyright © 2022 by Albert Whitman & Company
Illustrations by Rea Zhai
First published in the United States of America
in 2022 by Albert Whitman & Company
ISBN 978-0-8075-3168-6 (hardcover)
ISBN 978-0-8075-3169-3 (ebook)

Printed in China
10 9 8 7 6 5 4 3 2 1 WKT 26 25 24 23 22 21

Design by Valerie Hernández

For more information about Albert Whitman & Company,
visit our website at www.albertwhitman.com.

My house was like the middle of an old sandwich, squished and dark and icky.
Sometimes I didn't like being there.

Like this morning, when Dad found ants in the kitchen,
and he got really mad at us,
like it was our fault that the ants marched in.

He slammed the door
so hard the glass broke.

Dad was the strongest thing—
and I knew that when he came back,
he'd yell that the broken glass in the door
was our fault too.

So my shoulders sank like a ship,
and my belly squirmed with worry.

Mom whispered, "Love you, Sera,"
before I climbed onto the bus.
I looked back to say, "Love you too,"
but I knew I'd cry if I said it.
So I puffed my chest
and stomped up the steps.

My bus driver, Diggy, said, "Step softer, Seraphina,
or we'll have to build a new way to get off this bus."
His silliness felt good.

Once my house looked

too small for me to fit back inside it,

I laughed and joked with Carter and Meera.

My school stood like a shining castle on the hill,
big and bright and cheery.

I rushed to see my nice teacher
and my funny friends
and our colorful classroom

where we sang songs
and learned lessons
and ate the best snacks,
thanks to Mr. Keef.

But when Mr. Keef said,
"The school day's halfway over, kiddos!"
my shoulders sank like a ship,
and my belly squirmed with worry.

Then I stomped
and bumped
and broke,

during recess

and library

and science.

Over and over, Mr. Keef asked,
"Sera, is something wrong?"

"No!" I said back
in my strongest voice.

During art, I started painting the happiest house.

The hallway got noisy,
but I kept painting anyway.

I heard Mr. Keef ask Ignacio to close
the classroom door.
But he slammed it so hard and
so loud that I squeezed my eyes shut.

And I thought about the door
at home and the broken glass
that was going to be my fault.

I opened my eyes, and my painting
looked dripped and messed and ruined.
Mad swirled in my mind.
I gritted my teeth
and breathed like an angry bull.
Then I stomped over,
with my finger straight out.

And I pushed it close to Ignacio's face
and screamed,
"Look what you did!
This is all your fault!!"
For a second, I felt like the strongest thing.

Ignacio spoke in a soft voice. "Sera, I didn't mean it."

He looked up at me with watery eyes...

and I didn't feel so strong,

'cause I knew how he felt: scared.

My eyes filled with tears.

I was acting like my bully at home...

My bully that yelled

and screamed

and hurt.

So I shook my head and cried the words I wanted Dad to say to me:

"I'm so sorry."

Then I hid behind Carter and waited for Mr. Keef to yell at me.

But he stayed nice.
He bent down and asked,
"Do you want to talk after school? Can I help?"
I nodded.

Then my friends hugged me tight,
and everyone gathered around.

And I knew that the strongest thing
could never be loud and scary and angry,
because the strongest thing was calm
and kind
and so much stronger...

Just like me.